TEEN TITANS™
VOLCANO POWER

by Jack Oliver
Illustrated by Joe Staton and Mike DeCarlo, with color by Lee Loughridge

SCHOLASTIC INC.

New York   Toronto   London   Auckland   Sydney

Mexico City   New Delhi   Hong Kong   Buenos Aires

© 2005 DC Comics
TEEN TITANS and all related characters and elements are
trademarks of DC Comics © 2005. All rights reserved.

Published by Scholastic Inc. SCHOLASTIC and associated logos
are trademarks and/or registered trademarks of Scholastic Inc.

ISBN 0-439-75475-5
Designed by Henry Ng

12 11 10 9 8 7 6 5 4 3 2 1   5 6 7 8 9/0

Printed in the U.S.A.
First printing, November 2005

After Robin's flying dunk, the Teen Titans' basketball game was tied. The next basket would decide the winner.

"Thanks for the lift, Cyborg!" Robin called to his teammate.

SCORE
10
10

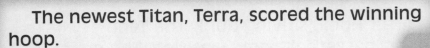

The newest Titan, Terra, scored the winning hoop.

"Rematch!" hollered Cyborg.

"You rock, Terra!" yelled Beast Boy.

"A most excellent play!" Starfire cheered.

The celebration was cut short when Robin received a message on his T-Communicator. "There's been a break-in at the museum," he said. "Teen Titans—go!"

"Smoke!" yelled Robin, "I thought you were in jail."

"Let's just say an old friend set me free," said Smoke. "Now I'm back to make some money, starting with these jewels. This jetpack isn't cheap, you know!"

The villain dodged Raven's magic, Robin's Birdarang, and Beast Boy's tentacles. "He turns to smoke before we can hit him," said Robin.

"You know the old saying, Titans," joked Smoke.
"*Where there's smoke, there's fire!*"
"Beast Boy, Starfire, watch out!" shouted Cyborg.

Beast Boy morphed into an elephant and squirted out the flames.

Meanwhile, Terra collapsed a wall of rocks to block the fire from reaching Starfire. "Thank you for your timely creation," said Starfire.

While the Titans dealt with the fire, Smoke found what he had been seeking—an ancient treasure map! "This will lead me to all the gold I'll ever need," he said with a smile.

"Sorry, buddy," said Cyborg. "No smoking allowed in the museum."

"Titans, let's take him down!" yelled Robin. "Wait!" cried Terra, as a pain shot through her head. "I'm losing control of my powers."

The rock wall above Smoke exploded outward. Terra tried to pull the rocks back to repair the wall, but the hole just got bigger.

"Thanks for the perfect escape hatch, Titans!" Smoke said. "It appears that you're good for something after all." He dove through the hole and his jetpack ignited, thrusting him out of sight.

"I've ruined everything," said Terra. "It's my fault Smoke got away. Maybe the Titans would be better off without me."

"We need you to help catch Smoke," said Beast Boy. "Plus, without you today, who would have saved Starfire?"

The Titans returned to their tower to discuss plans for capturing Smoke.

"According to the museum," explained Robin, "the map Smoke stole leads to an ancient treasure in a cave on Volcano Island."

"Did you just say *volcano*?" asked Beast Boy.

"It's a dormant volcano," said Robin. "It hasn't erupted in years."

"Why doesn't that make me feel better?" asked Raven.

The Titans arrived on Volcano Island in search of Smoke.

"How are we supposed to find Smoke if he has the map?" asked Cyborg.

"Let's see what I can spy with eagle's eyes," said Beast Boy.

"I see the volcano in the distance," said Starfire.

"There's black smoke all around it," said Raven. "Follow me."

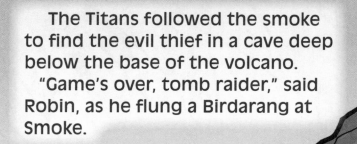

The Titans followed the smoke to find the evil thief in a cave deep below the base of the volcano.

"Game's over, tomb raider," said Robin, as he flung a Birdarang at Smoke.

Using his jetpack, Smoke escaped from the cave, but left the heavy gold behind. With a few well-placed giant boulders, Terra made sure he didn't escape the island.

23

Raven used her powers to push back Smoke's deadly fire blasts.

"You can't defeat me, Titans!" said Smoke. "I'm too strong!"

The volcano began to erupt, oozing hot lava from its crater.

"Terra, stay focused!" cried Beast Boy. "The volcano's erupting!"

At Robin's signal, the Titans split up. With help from Beast Boy, Robin snuck up behind Smoke while he was still busy fighting Raven.

Without his jetpack, Smoke crashed to the ground. Raven quickly bound him with an energy cord.

"You're not so tough now, Smoke," said Robin.

"Maybe you should change your name to *Fumes*," added Raven.

The other Titans were busy stopping the erupting volcano.
"I can't hold the lava back much longer!" cried Starfire.

"I can," said Terra. She clogged the volcano's crater, blocking more lava from escaping.

"Way to go, Terra," said Beast Boy. "You stopped the volcano."

"She kind of started it, too," said Raven.

"But in the end, she controlled her powers," argued Beast Boy. "She saved us all."

"Thanks, Beast Boy!" said Terra. She gave him a big hug.

"Let's get this treasure to the museum," said Robin.
"And let's take Smoke to his jail cell," Starfire added.
"I wonder who freed him," said Cyborg.

As the other Titans headed home, Terra hung back on the island.

"Only I can help you control your powers," a familiar voice told her.

"I'll never join forces with you," Terra insisted.

"We shall see, Terra," the evil voice replied. "We shall see."